# Catty Corner

## POUNCES INTO ACTION

JULIE MURPHY

ART BY EVE FARB

union square kids

NEW YORK

For Teagan, the queen of catnaps.

# CHAPTER ONE

Catty Corner was so good at school that she was practically an expert. If there was something to know about Friends Hollow Elementary, Catty knew it.

She knew where the coldest water fountain was and how many flakes to feed the class pet fish, Douglas Snickerdoodle. She knew which swing in the playground swung the highest, and she knew that Fish Taco Tuesday was the best day to

eat cafeteria food. She also knew that her teacher, Mr. Grole, liked to listen to classical music during reading time, and that her best friend Bebe was always fashionably late for school, while her *other* best friend Jo believed that if you weren't ten minutes early, you were tardy.

Catty had even mastered Mom and Dad's big three rules: no hissing, no scratching, no biting. She was the most Zen half-cat, half-girl in all of Friends Hollow. Not even Rufus, the grumpy neighbor cat, could get under her claws.

It did help that she had a very special diary passed down from Granny Tabby to Mom and now to Catty. It was lavender and fuzzy with the words SCRATCH PAD stitched across the front. Not only could Catty take out her feelings and go all cattywampus on the pages inside, but if she ever needed to sink her claws into something, the soft fluffy cover was just right.

It also helped to have friends like Jo and Bebe, who were so different and still totally made sense. It was like salted caramel, or pizza and ranch, or tuna salad and cheese doodles. (Okay, that last combo might be one that only Catty liked.) The girls rode the bus together in the morning, sat together in class, played together at recess, and took the bus home again at the end of the day. They had a routine, and Catty liked routines.

"What is a group of cats called?" Jo asked Catty one Thursday before their afternoon volunteer period with the preschoolers.

"Oh, I'm not sure," said Catty. Cats didn't hang out together very often, as far as Catty knew. "I guess a colony?"

"A colony of cats?" said Bebe.

"Maybe we're a *pounce*," Catty said, thinking of her favorite thing to do.

"Me-ow!" Jo said, laughing. "But Catty, we're not cats!"

Catty snorted. "That's okay. I won't hold it against you."

"Pounce," Bebe said. "I like the sound of that."

Jo shrugged. "Then I guess that makes us a pounce!"

When the bell rang, the girls pounced on the opportunity to visit the preschoolers. As third-graders, Catty, Bebe, and Jo were all official Big Kid Helpers for Mrs. Macaw's preschool class across the hall.

Catty liked helping the preschoolers, even though sometimes they forgot not to tug on her tail or not to shout in her extra-sensitive ears.

Just as the girls were about to knock, Mrs. Macaw's door swung open.

There stood one of their favorite preschoolers, Sandy, and she was in tears. "Catty! Bebe! Jo!" She hiccupped. "Something terrible has happened!"

Catty was worried, but then again, preschoolers could be *so* dramatic. Maybe someone used Sandy's favorite crayon or wore a shirt that was "too purple."

But it wasn't anything so simple.

"It's . . . it's . . . !" Sandy gasped.

"It's okay, Sandy," said Catty. "Sometimes when I'm about to go cattywampus, I take three deep breaths to calm down. We can do it together. Ready? One—"

"It's our *macaroniiiiiiiiiiiiiii!*" Sandy moaned and collapsed into Catty's arms.

"Mac Aroney? Never heard of him!" said Jo with a chuckle.

"Is this a culinary emergency, Sandy?" asked Bebe, whose mother was a chef and owned a local restaurant, Penne a la Wanda.

"No, it's our macaroni sculptures!" said Sandy. "They're *ruined!*"

Every year, with the help of their Big Kid Helpers, the preschoolers made macaroni sculptures for their parents. And this year, the sculptures had taken a lot of time and *a lot* of patience . . . especially from the Big Kid Helpers. In fact, just the other night, Catty had a nightmare she was being chased by a giant box of ziti . . .

The girls followed Sandy inside Mrs. Macaw's classroom—and gasped. Maybe Sandy wasn't being dramatic. It was a cat-astrophe! Broken macaroni and shredded construction paper were everywhere, along with spilled paint and glitter. *Lots* of glitter.

*Oooh! Shiny!* thought Catty, but she quickly composed herself.

"Avert your eyes!" Jo said, covering Sandy's eyes with her hands. "It's too horrible!"

"But I've already seen it!" said Sandy.

"Oh yeah . . ." said Jo.

"What happened?" asked Catty.

"We don't know!" said Sandy. "It was like this when we got here this morning!"

“This is like that time my sister and I made mac and cheese in my mom’s stand mixer,” said Jo. “We turned it on and *whoosh*! Macaroni wall art! My mom was like—”

Jo kept talking, but Catty tuned her out. The way Jo told stories, you never knew where they were going, and usually neither did Jo. Instead, Catty tried to concentrate on the problem at hand. She listened hard and twitched her ears. There was something funny in the air . . . and it wasn’t glitter *or* Jo’s story.

Mrs. Macaw came up to them. She looked frazzled, but that was nothing new.

“Mrs. Macaw, you have macaroni in your hair,” Bebe said helpfully.

“Thank you, Bebe,” sighed Mrs. Macaw.

"I'm glad you're here, girls. It's been a chaotic morning."

"Who would ruin all these macaroni sculptures?" Catty couldn't imagine anyone would be mean enough to wreck them on purpose.

"Could it have been a ghost?" asked Jo.

"Perhaps someone desperately needed to make a casserole," said Bebe, scratching her chin.

Those were interesting suggestions, but Catty wasn't so sure. She had something her friends didn't: a fantastically sensitive kitty nose. And right about then it was working overtime. Catty sniffed. She snuffed. She took three quick snorts and then one long *snaaaarf*! Hmm. Over the fruity glue sticks and musty well-loved stuffed animals, she sensed . . . something. *Something that didn't belong.* Catty's nose twitched.

"Whoever it was, they left a funny smell," she said.

"I don't care *who* or *what* it was," Sandy wailed. "I'm just too . . . too . . . saaAAAAAaaad!"

Sandy fell into Catty's arms again. "Don't worry, Sandy," said Catty. "We'll help you rebuild your macaroni sculptures. Right, guys?"

Jo and Bebe nodded. They did everything together, after all. "That's right!" they said.

"And this time, we won't even get glue in our hair!" Catty told her.

"You're the best Big Kid Helpers ever!" said Sandy. "I'm so relieved I could fall down all over again!"

And so, she did.

When Catty finally untangled herself from Sandy, she whispered to her friends, "Something fishy is going on here, and I don't mean like Bebe's mom's seared tuna and squid ink pasta. I think we need to investigate."

"I'm in!" said Jo.

"Indubitably!" said Bebe.

True to their word, Catty, Jo, and Bebe helped Sandy and the other preschoolers rebuild their macaroni sculptures. Catty only got distracted chasing glitter once or twice (okay, maybe five times), and soon the artwork was almost as good as new.

"Thank you so much, ladies!" Mrs. Macaw said when they were done.

"Mrs. Macaw, you've got macaroni stuck to your dress," said Bebe helpfully.

"Thank you, Bebe," sighed Mrs. Macaw.

"I've got an idea," Catty said, surveying their work. "Why don't we hang these sculptures up at the Meatball Mania fund-raising dinner tomorrow night?"

"Catty, that's ingenious!" said Bebe. "My mom would love it! She's always been a lover of fine art."

"I think that's a fabulous idea, Catty," said Mrs. Macaw.

Tomorrow night was the big Meatball Mania fundraising dinner in the school's cafeteria. This year, Bebe's mom was in charge, which meant Bebe, Catty, and Jo got to help out in the kitchen. The donations would buy more art supplies for the whole school. (Catty's suggestion had been a crinkly cat tunnel for the gymnasium, but she had to agree that art supplies were pretty cool too . . . )

With their work done, it was time to get their snack before heading to recess.

Catty liked helping out, but she was relieved to take a break from the preschoolers. Besides, sometimes Catty just wanted Bebe and Jo to herself. There was nothing better than snack time with her pounce.

*Especially* when Catty's mom had packed her favorite smoked herring—yum!

"I can't wait to try the fritters my mom packed," Bebe was saying. "They smelled *so good* this morning."

"Dad always packs a little bag of *just* lemon jelly beans, 'cause he knows those are my favorite," said Jo. "One time my sister and I tried to see how many we could shove up our noses, and boy, let me tell you—"

But Jo never got the chance to finish her story, because when the girls reached Mr. Grole's classroom, something made them freeze in horror. Catty's tail bushed straight out as if to say, *On guard!*

Tragedy had struck again, and this time it was more than macaroni.

# CHAPTER TWO

The snack pantry had been *ransacked*! The door was wide open, the floor littered with cookie crumbs, crumpled juice cartons, and lunch boxes cracked open like walnuts. Cracker dust, jelly smears, and half-nibbled raisins littered every shelf. And was that a celery stick embedded in the ceiling?

They'd been robbed! Someone had stolen their snacks!

Mr. Grole was surveying the pillaged goodies, shaking his big shaggy head. "Girls, I'm sorry you had to see this," he said.

"My herring's gone!" Catty moaned, turning over her own empty lunch bag.

"I'm so sorry, Catty," Mr. Grole said, even though Catty knew he didn't enjoy the smell. "Everyone's snacks are missing. Even my organic honey chews!"

Catty's nose twitched again. Something was odd here, and it wasn't just Mr. Grole's taste in candy.

"It must be the . . . Macaroni Marauder!" Bebe said.

"What's a marauder?" Jo asked.

"Like, a thief," Bebe said. "First they destroyed the macaroni sculptures, then they had our snacks for dessert!" Bebe

Meatball Mania

gasped. "What if they go after the spaghetti for the fundraising dinner next? My mom's dropping the food off this afternoon!"

Now Bebe looked like she might collapse into someone's arms. Catty braced herself.

"Now, girls, I don't think anything malicious is going on," Mr. Grole said.

"That's because all our malicious snacks have been stolen!" moaned Jo.

"Not 'delicious,' '*malicious*,'" said Mr. Grole. "It means 'bad or mean on purpose.' I'm sure whatever happened to our snacks was just an accident."

An *accident*? The girls looked at one another with raised eyebrows. Catty wasn't sure she believed this was an accident. First Mrs. Macaw's macaroni, then Mr. Grole's snack pantry. What would be next?

The girls made their way outside, hoping to make the most of a *very* hungry recess.

"Rats!" Jo said. "I was really looking forward to my snack."

"No, not rats," said Bebe, who seemed lost in thought. "Mice! My mom had mice at her restaurant one time. They got into everything and made a mess, just like in the snack pantry. The health inspector shut her down for a whole weekend. She was devastated! Now she cleans *everything* three times. At least!"

"I don't know," Catty said. One of Catty's best friends was a mouse named Waffles, but he was made of felt. As a half-cat, Catty knew *plenty* about real mice, especially their smell. She hadn't smelled any mousey friends in Mrs. Macaw's classroom, or in Mr. Grole's snack pantry. If there were mice anywhere nearby, Catty would know.

"It has to be the Gobbler Bandit," Jo said. "My dad teaches history at the college, and way back in the day, all the grain stores in town started disappearing . . ."

"Oh, Jo, not another story," groaned Bebe.

Normally, Catty might agree with Bebe, but this seemed important.

"Jo, what were you saying?" Catty urged.

"The Gobbler Bandit!" said Jo. "Once the candy shop downtown was cleared out, then another time all the local delis were cleaned out overnight. They never caught the thief, but they called him the Gobbler Bandit! Or at least, um, that's what I think he's called." Jo smiled sheepishly.

"Well, if charcuterie was stolen, then it was *obviously* mice!" Bebe snapped. "Mice *love* charcuterie! Everyone knows that!"

"They do not!"

"They do too!"

Uh-oh. This conversation was going all cattywampus. "Pouncers!" Catty said, her ears pointing straight up the way they did when she meant business. "We're not going to solve this problem by squabbling."

This seemed to snap them out of it. *Phew!*

"We need to get our snacks back, and save Meatball Mania, right?" Catty asked.

"Indubitably!" said Bebe.

Just then, Milo, a boy in Catty's grade, was strolling by. Milo lived across the street from Catty and liked the same series of books she did. But he could also be a little rude.

"Hey! What are you three whispering about?" Milo asked, hefting the big backpack he lugged around everywhere.

Jo put her hands on her hips and stood toe to toe with Milo. "The snack pantry was robbed. Do you happen to know anything about that?"

Milo held his hands up. "No way! I was in the library. Wait, did you say *robbed*? I just got a detective kit for my birthday. This would be the perfect time to use it."

"The preschoolers also had their macaroni art wrecked," Bebe told him. "You didn't see anyone go in there, did you, Milo?"

Catty rolled her eyes. All she wanted was to solve this mystery with her friends.

The last thing she needed was Milo's help. He definitely wasn't part of their pounce.

"It's no big deal, really," Catty said, hoping Bebe and Jo would get the hint, and Milo would get lost. Didn't they remember how mean he'd been to Catty when she first came to school? Sure, he was a little nicer now, but no way was she going to trust him with top-secret information. "We'll see you on the playground, Milo."

Milo frowned. "But—"

Catty corralled Jo and Bebe into the empty cafeteria and out of sight. There were already posters hanging for Meatball Mania: *You Want the Best? Why Settle for Less? Bring Your Family to Meatball Mania!* Catty wanted to make sure the dinner went well and made plenty of money for the art supplies, especially since the preschoolers had to use a bunch of extra materials to redo their sculptures. There probably wasn't even a speck of glitter left in this school.

When the door shut behind them, Catty looked her best friends in the eye. "There's a mystery afoot, and we're going to solve it."

"It's a mouse," Bebe said.

"It's a ghost," Jo said.

"Mouse!"

"Ghost!"

The two girls glared at each other.

"No hissing, no scratching, no biting!" Catty said.

"Huh?" said Bebe and Jo.

"They're my big three rules for school. But they apply here too, okay? Fighting isn't going to get us anywhere," Catty told them. "I don't know who's responsible, but we're not going to find out—"

"We're not?" Jo asked.

"Unless . . . we work together. Right?" Catty grinned, then put her hand out into the circle between them. "Paws in!"

Bebe and Jo gave each other stern looks before finally nodding.

"Three, two, one," they chanted together. "Let's pounce!"

# CHAPTER THREE

"Let's start at the scene of the crime," Catty said as Bebe and Jo followed her back to Mr. Grole's room. They could hear the rest of their classmates playing outside, but there was no time for games when perfectly good snacks were going missing and Meatball Mania was at stake!

"But wait, aren't we supposed to be at recess?" asked Bebe.

"We're being sneaky," said Catty. "But it's for a good cause!"

"And no one will know if we're super quiet!" shouted Jo.

"Shhh!" said Catty and Bebe.

"Oh, right! Sorry."

The snack pantry at the back of the classroom was still a mess. There were wrappers and crumbs and half-eaten snacks everywhere, as if a really hungry tornado had just blown through.

Catty stepped close to the pantry and began to sniff. "I think I might be able to smell some clues," she explained now that she had a chance to concentrate.

Bebe held up a granola bar. "These teeth marks look very mouselike," she said.

"Let me see that," said Jo, reaching for the snack. But just then the girls heard footsteps coming down the hallway.

Catty tugged them both behind the pantry door. She held a finger to her lips.

Bebe and Jo nodded, even though Jo looked like she might burst if she didn't get to talk about the granola bar.

Catty held her breath as she watched through the crack in the door.

"It's Mr. Hobbs, the janitor," Jo whispered in the loudest whisper voice of all time. "Every year for Christmas he puts lights on his janitor cart and plays Christmas music. One time I asked him if he takes requests and he said no one had ever asked, but that he would be happy to."

Behind her, Bebe rolled her eyes. Catty was starting to get a little annoyed too.

Mr. Hobbs wheeled his cart into the classroom to empty Mr. Grole's trash can.

But Jo kept on going. "So I asked him to play 'Dominic the Donkey,' and he said he'd never heard of that song and I was like, 'Say what!' because 'Dominic—' "

"Shhhh!" went Catty.

Jo covered her mouth with her hand and nodded.

Mr. Hobbs froze, then glanced around the classroom. Catty could practically hear her own heart beating like a drum in her chest. If Mr. Hobbs caught them, would they get in trouble? Would he think *they* stole the snacks? But then Mr. Hobbs returned to his task and whistled as he wheeled his cart back out into the hallway. All three girls relaxed.

"We should keep the door shut in case anyone else walks by," Bebe said.

"Good call," said Catty. But with the door shut it was awfully hard to see.

"Does anyone have a flashlight?" Jo asked. "I'm, uh, not what you would call a fan of the dark."

"I can see in the dark," Catty told her.

"You can?" said Jo.

"Cat vision," Catty said with a smile. "Oh, but I guess that isn't much help to you two."

Jo frowned. "Yeah, but that's pretty cool."

"I think I have a mini flashlight in my emergency bag," Bebe said.

"Oooooh," Jo said. "What else do you have in that thing?"

"Mainly gum, hair ties, and lip balm. Oh, and tiny condiments like hot sauce and salt and pepper!" said Bebe. "Just in case a dish needs a little extra flavor."

She dug around in her backpack for a minute, before—*CLICK!* The pantry was illuminated with her tiny hot pink flashlight.

Jo held her hands to her eyes. "Ahh, I'm blind!"

She shrugged when Catty and Bebe didn't laugh. "Okay, what are we looking for?"

"I wonder if the types of food that were taken are clues," Bebe said. "Maybe the mice are working on some kind of recipe . . ."

"Well, I'm pretty sure ghosts don't eat," said Jo, "so I don't think they would even try to make food."

Catty closed her eyes and tried to let her sense of smell do the work. At home, they never had a mouse problem because Mom could smell the mice before they even had a chance to nibble.

"If ghosts don't eat, why are they stealing macaroni and snacks?" asked Bebe. "What we really need is someone with detective equipment."

"Like Milo?" Catty asked. "No way that's happening."

Jo peeked into a mangled box of animal crackers. "Sometimes ghosts just like to play tricks. Or maybe they just really miss food. But ghosts aren't my only theory!"

It was so noisy that Catty couldn't think straight. She tried to listen carefully. Maybe Bebe was right, and it really was mice. She thought she'd smelled something like a rodent. But if Catty could just hear them scratching . . .

Jo tapped the side of her head. "You know, what I really think we have on our hands is the Gobbler Bandit! My dad told me about one time last year when someone broke into Flaky's Bakery downtown and stole all their raspberry donuts. Can you imagine eating fifty raspberry donuts? I hear the Gobbler Bandit has a serious sweet tooth."

Bebe shined her flashlight into every dark corner. "I could really use Milo's detective kit right about now."

Catty was trying so hard to concentrate that she barely even heard Bebe.

Jo groaned. "Not Milo!"

Bebe smiled nervously. "I know he's a little bit of a pain, but Milo could be a really big help with his detective tools."

"NO WAY!" Jo and Catty said in unison.

Jo threw her arms up. "What if we invited him to help and he just gave us all wet willies the whole time?"

"Or what if he yanks my tail?" Catty asked.

"Yeah! We all know what happened the last time someone messed with your tail," Jo said.

"Eeeek!" Bebe said. The last time some-one stepped on Catty's tail, Catty had accidentally bitten Bebe. It wasn't a moment either girl wanted to repeat.

"Hey! That was an accident!" said Catty.

All three girls talked over each other, airing their own opinions of Milo, the thief, and what should be done. It all made Catty's tail bristle. They were a pounce! They were supposed to work together!

There was no use for Catty to even try to sniff or hear her way around this pantry now. Any chance of concentrating in peace was history!

Just then, the door to the classroom flew open. All three girls shrieked. Catty was so surprised, she jumped straight up and clung to the shelf by her claws.

Meatball Mania

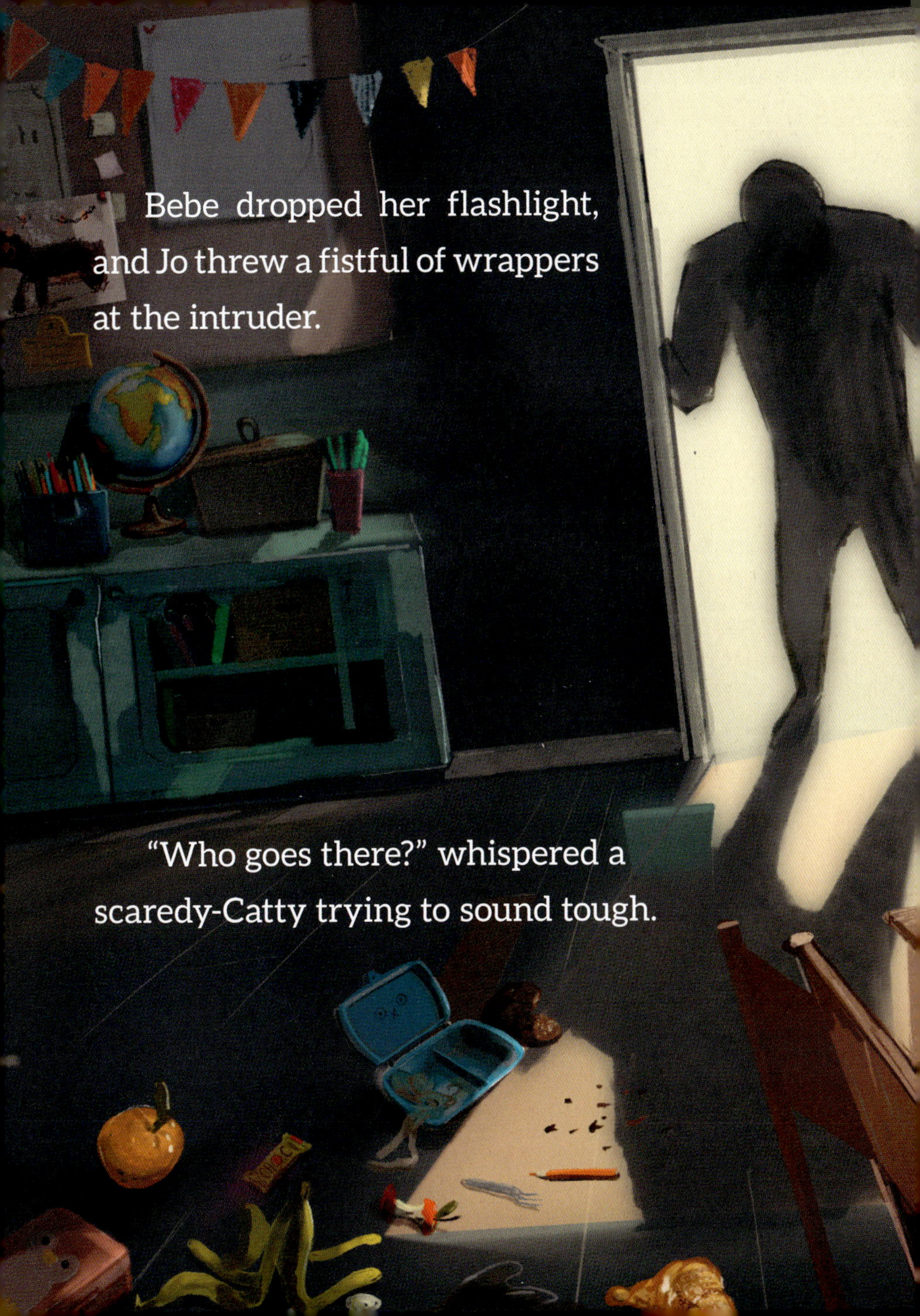

Bebe dropped her flashlight, and Jo threw a fistful of wrappers at the intruder.

"Who goes there?" whispered a scaredy-Catty trying to sound tough.

Then the looming figure in the door stepped forward so the girls could see that it was just Mr. Grole.

"What are you three doing in here?" he grumbled.

"Uh-oh," Jo said. "Are we in trouble?"

Catty fell to the ground with a thud.

"Girls, I think it's time to get to recess," he said as he stepped aside to let them out of the room.

Bebe crossed her arms and stomped off past Mr. Grole with Catty and Jo close behind.

"Bebe, are you okay?" Catty asked. Bebe seemed furious.

"It's time to stop playing around," she said. "No more silly theories about ghosts or Gobbler Bandits. If we don't get this thing figured out, the whole spaghetti dinner could be ruined!"

"That's what we're trying to do!" said Jo. "Why don't you go hang out with Milo, if you think he's so special!"

And with that, Jo huffed and walked off toward the swing set while Bebe headed toward the sandbox, her ponytail swinging.

What just happened?

Catty stood there by herself, no best friends, no pounce. Suddenly she was all alone, just like the first days at school before Jo and Bebe became her forever besties. Except now there was a mouse or a ghost or a Gobbler Bandit on the loose.

If Jo and Bebe weren't going to help, it was up to Catty to solve the mystery and save the day.

Maybe only a cat could catch a mouse.

# CHAPTER FOUR

"I think I better go home instead of coming over today, Jo," Bebe said as they all walked to the bus. "My mom's been working so hard on this spaghetti dinner, and I really need to figure out who or what is behind all this mischief. Could you imagine if the meatballs went missing? It would be so tragic for my mom's restaurant. Besides, you can't have Meatball Mania without the meatballs!"

Catty frowned. "I just feel so bad for the preschoolers." Her tummy growled. "And for myself, honestly. I never skip my afternoon snack."

The girls had planned to go to Jo's house and make signs for the fundraising dinner, but after that afternoon at the snack pantry, maybe it was a good idea for Bebe to have a little space from the pounce. Sometimes Catty and Waffles needed a little space from each other, but that was usually when he was giving her the silent treatment.

"Bebe, are you okay?" Catty asked.

Bebe didn't answer and put on her headphones. When they got off the bus, Jo led the way in the opposite direction of Catty's house.

But Bebe just did a small wave and walked in the other direction.

Jo shrugged. "Come on, Catty."

Catty followed, but her tail drooped.

After turning the corner, the two friends stopped in front of a narrow two-story house with tons of yard decorations. There were flamingos and a giant rooster and a tire swing that didn't look very reliable. The grass was a little tall, and the flower beds were full of more weeds than flowers. The house was painted a bright green with hot pink trim. It all looked much wilder than Catty's house, and Jo's family weren't even half-cat!

Jo flung her arms in the air. "Home sweet home." She turned to Catty. "My parents think yard work is boring, and they're totally right. Come on! I can't wait for you to meet everyone."

“Everyone?” Catty asked as she skipped over the cracks in the sidewalk.

The moment Jo opened the door, the sounds in her house hit Catty like a freight train. Her ears stood at attention, as she stumbled backwards a little bit before following Jo inside.

“I’m home!” Jo yelled over the noise from the television and three of her brothers jumping on the couch. “And the Gobbler Bandit is on the loose!”

The boys screamed in response before going back to their jumping.

“That’s Jason, Jory, and Jack,” Jo said. Then she pointed to a family portrait on the wall with nine kids, two adults, and one parakeet. “They’re two years younger than me. But there’s also Janessa and Jacob.

They're the babies. And then my older siblings are Jacqueline, Jordan, and Jody."

"Your parents must like the letter 'J' a lot. Is that your bird?" Catty asked, practically yelling over the noise.

"Yup! Her name is Hot Dog."

"No J name?" Catty wondered aloud.

"Mom wanted to name her Jasmine, but the kids voted and Hot Dog won. I was personally pulling for Bunny. A bird named Bunny! How funny would that be?"

Catty had to admit that would have been sort of funny. "Where should we make signs?" she asked.

Overhead, there was a loud smash followed by crashes and thuds.

"Sorry!" Jo yelled. "That's Jordan! She's practicing on her drums!"

Catty cringed. Loud, surprising noises did not make for a calm kitty. Her fingers ached to claw right through something. Too bad her journal was in her bag at the front door. It would look weird to take it out and go a little cattywampus on the fuzzy cover to ease her nerves.

Just then, a tall woman with light pink curly hair stumbled out into the living room carrying a giant laundry basket of towels. "The washing machine at the salon broke!" she said. "And I've got to get these all washed and dried before I open tomorrow!"

"Catty, this is my mom," Jo said.

The woman dropped the basket so she could see. "Oh! Hello there! Lovely hair, truly. And those ears! What I wouldn't give to style you!"

"Mom!" Jo said.

"Your hair is lovely, too, honey."

"Yeah, right." Jo scowled. "Every time I leave the house without brushing my hair, my mom says I'm a walking advertisement for her hair salon."

Catty blushed at the attention. The only haircut she'd ever had was at home in her kitchen from her mom. But Jo's mom seemed pretty funky and fun—even if she did make Catty want to find the nearest scratching post and go to town. "Thanks, Mrs.—"

"Call me Mama J!" she said. "Jo, honey, I'm going to need your help with these towels as soon as possible."

"Last time I did laundry, I used quadruple soap—you know, so everything would be cleaner? Well, the machine overflowed and there were soapsuds everywhere!" Jo told her.

Mama J spun around to head back to the kitchen. "Consider it a learning experience! Besides, the basement floor had never been cleaner!"

Catty looked to Jo once her mom had left the room. "Your mom is—"

"My dad calls her the Queen of Chaos." Jo spread her arms out. "And this is her kingdom. Come on! I want to show you something in my dad's study before he gets home."

Catty chased Jo upstairs. The whole house was basically an obstacle course! Catty leapt over and wove around boxes and piles of blocks and even a kid or two just to get to the top of the stairs. The long hallway was pounding with drums and several different types of loud music. Catty could hardly think! How could Jo live with all this mayhem?

At the end of the hallway, Jo opened a door to a room so small it could have been a closet, but it had a desk big enough for writing and bookshelves from floor to ceiling. But best of all, it was quiet!

Jo closed the door and it was like the two girls were in a safe little bubble.

Catty sighed with relief. She could really use a catnap right about now!

"It should be around here somewhere," Jo said as she began to climb the wobbly ladder to reach the upper shelves. It looked sort of fun. If Catty ever came back over to

Jo's, this was definitely the room she'd want to hang out in.

"Aha!" Jo said, and practically slid down the ladder.

Jo held up a book for Catty to see called *Local Legends of Friends Hollow*. "My dad used this book in his local history class at the college."

Catty watched over Jo's shoulder as she flipped through the pages before landing on the chapter she was looking for. The title read "The Gobbler Bandit: The Thief Who Ate the Evidence."

"Whoa," Catty managed to say as Jo flipped the page to reveal an illustration of a person in a black and gray striped shirt, with puffy white hair and a black eye mask.

Local Legends
of Friendly Hollow

"You really think it could be the Gobbler Bandit?" Catty asked. She'd finally begun to calm down from all the noise and sensations in Jo's house.

Jo nodded with wide eyes. "I wouldn't be surprised if this guy or his *ghost* shows up tomorrow and eats every last bit of spaghetti before—"

The door flung open and a vacuum zoomed between Catty's feet. She jumped so high in the air that she didn't even need a ladder to reach the top shelf. Catty's poor tail looked like she'd been electrocuted, and her ears ached at the sound of the vacuum combined with the music, the drums, and the unbelievably loud television downstairs.

Jo's mom hummed to herself. "Don't mind me! Just coming through!"

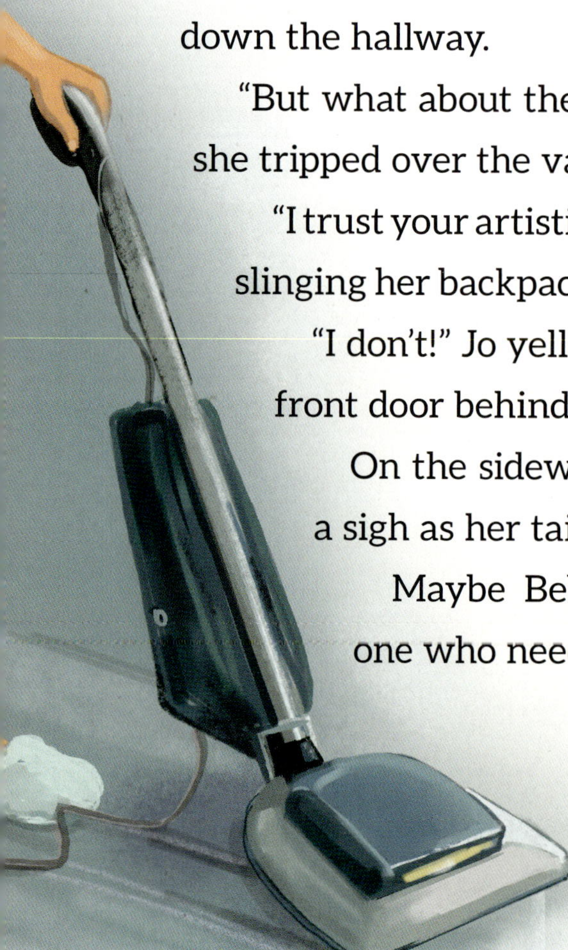

Catty felt like she would claw her way up the bookshelf if she didn't get out of there.

"I gotta go!" Catty called as she dashed down the hallway.

"But what about the signs?" Jo asked as she tripped over the vacuum cord.

"I trust your artistic vision!" Catty said, slinging her backpack over her shoulder.

"I don't!" Jo yelled as Catty shut the front door behind her.

On the sidewalk, Catty breathed a sigh as her tail relaxed.

Maybe Bebe wasn't the only one who needed some space.

# CHAPTER FIVE

All Catty wanted was to curl up in bed with Waffles for *maximum chill time*. Maybe she'd even put her headphones on and listen to soothing bird-chirping sounds. But when she got home, there was a note waiting for her on her front door.

*Mom is nervous about her spaghetti sauce recipe, and we need another taste tester. Could you please come help when you get home? You're our only hope!*

*Fashionably yours,*

*Bebe*

After reading the note, Catty set out for Bebe's house on the other end of the street. She couldn't leave a friend in peril! Besides, Bebe's mom was a fantastic cook and always made something delicious.

As she was crossing the road, Catty noticed Milo watching her through his blinds. As soon as she saw him, he ducked! And he'd called *Catty* a weirdo? Milo wasn't

Catty's favorite person, but what if his detective kit really could help?

To be honest, Catty felt pretty cool that Bebe thought her opinion mattered enough to weigh in on the sauce. But as soon as she stopped in front of Bebe's house, that confidence melted away.

Bebe's house was a perfectly rectangular bright white building with a glossy red door and circle windows. It reminded Catty of weird paintings she'd seen in books that looked cool but didn't always make sense. Dad called it modern.

Bebe's lawn looked like someone had come out there with scissors and cut each blade of grass one by one. If Jo's house was wild, Bebe's house seemed far too tame.

When Bebe answered the door, she wore a white apron and matching chef's hat. "You're here! We need you to break a tie!" She pulled Catty inside and then pointed at the shoe rack by the door. "You can leave your sneakers there. Mom has a strict no-shoes rule."

Catty nodded. But her toes curled as she remembered that not only did her socks not match today, but one of them had a hole right on the big toe.

"Did you have any new ideas about the mystery thief?" Bebe asked in a whisper.

Catty shook her head. "We . . . I mean, I . . ." Catty wasn't sure if Bebe would want to hear about what Catty and Jo did without her. "Not really," she said.

"I think I have an idea for how we can investigate, but we can talk about that later," said Bebe. "Come on, my mom's waiting for us."

Bebe took Catty into the kitchen, where a tall, thin woman with jet-black hair stood with her eyes closed over two huge pots of simmering spaghetti sauce. She sniffed once, then twice.

"One of them has too much pepper. I can smell it," Bebe's mom said. "I just can't *taste* it."

"Mom?" Bebe asked, as if she was a little nervous to interrupt the moment her mom was having with the sauce. "This is Catty, my friend I was telling you about."

Bebe's mom spun around, a wooden spoon in her hand. "Catty, lovely to meet you. Oh, you're a cat person. How unique." She shook Catty's hand. "You may call me Chef Wanda or just Chef if you prefer."

"She has me call her Chef, too," Bebe whispered. "At least in the kitchen."

Chef Wanda glanced down at the hole in Catty's sock, then at the bit of fluff that had fallen from Catty's tail and landed on the clean white kitchen floor.

"Oh, uh," said Catty, embarrassed. "Sorry about that. I shed." She picked up the fluff and handed it awkwardly to Chef Wanda, who placed it in a trash can.

"That's quite all right, Catty. The thing is, I need your help, girls." Chef Wanda gestured to the simmering pots on the stove. "These sauces have become quite the dilemma, and I can't decide which would be the perfect match for my meatballs tomorrow night."

Bebe handed Catty a fresh wooden spoon and then an apron and hat of her own. "Chef specializes in haute cuisine, so she's a little nervous about making spaghetti and meatballs for the whole school."

"I thought spaghetti and meatballs were also served hot?" said Catty.

"Not 'hot,' '*haute*,'" said Chef Wanda, pronouncing the word with an accent. "It's French. It means 'fashionably elegant.'"

"Oh," said Catty.

Chef Wanda stood back from the stove so the girls could approach the sauce and give their feedback. Catty's stomach rumbled. She doubted she'd be able to taste the difference between the two sauces, but she'd give it a try. Both of them smelled incredibly good.

"Everything needs to be just perfect tomorrow," Chef Wanda explained. "What if someone doesn't like their meal and then they refuse to come to my restaurant?" She gasped. "Or worse: What if they write me a one-star review? The horror!"

"Catty has amazing taste," Bebe said.

"I do?" Catty asked. Sure, her dad was a recipe tester for the Friends Hollow Pie Company. But what if his talents hadn't passed on to her? She got her half-cat side from Mom.

Then Bebe leaned in and whispered, "I'm pretty sure the sauces are the exact same, but the woman is spiraling here. Plus, you do totally have good taste!"

"Okay, girls, get to sampling," Chef Wanda said.

Catty and Bebe took turns tasting spoonfuls of each sauce. When it was Catty's turn to try the second sauce, she accidentally scooped up a little too much. She held her hand as steady as possible as she brought the spoon to her mouth, but then Catty felt a tickle. There was a tingle in her nose. Maybe there really *was* too much pepper in the sauce, because all of a sudden Catty *sneezed.* And this was no ordinary sneeze. It was a gale-force, five-alarm sinus explosion. Sauce spattered all over the shiny stove and bright white cabinets.

Chef Wanda gasped as her hand flew to her chest. "Oh. My. That is quite the mess."

“I’m so sorry,” Catty said before licking the spoon.

Chef Wanda jumped into action, reaching for a mop and cleaning sprays and rags. "It's fine, it's fine. I'll just clean this up and then I can hear your thoughts. A clean kitchen is the most important utensil in any chef's cabinet."

"Mom," Bebe said, like she was a little embarrassed. "Sorry—I mean, Chef. It's just a little bit of sauce. I'll help you clean it up later."

Chef Wanda smiled tightly, like she'd just swallowed a mouse, as her fingers clenched around the mop. It reminded Catty of Dad when she messed with his collection of mini spoons. They all had a very specific place. To Catty, this house seemed like the kind of home where everything had to be just right, and between the hole in her sock and her atomic sneeze, Catty was far from just right. "Of course, we'll clean up later," said Chef Wanda, looking pained.

"I like them both," Catty told her as she nervously held her tail. "But I think the first one is missing that . . . oomph?"

Chef Wanda's eyes lit up. "I think you're on to something, Catty."

Catty stroked her tail, careful not to let any more fluff shed off onto Chef Wanda's clean floor.

"Now, Chef Bebe," said Chef Wanda. "I need my herbs and spices."

"Yes, Chef!" Bebe said, and hustled across the kitchen to a cabinet before returning with her arms full.

Chef Wanda studied the glass jars before plucking one out of the lineup.

Catty's jaw fell open and her eyes were bigger than meatballs. She recognized the dried green leaves in the jar immediately, and was so delighted she wanted to jump for joy. There was nothing Catty loved more than rolling in catnip, going a little cattywampus, and then snoozing in her favorite cat bed. She never would have guessed Bebe's family loved catnip too!

"Here, Catty, would you open this?" Chef Wanda asked, handing Catty the precious plant matter.

"Gladly!" said Catty, grabbing the jar from Chef Wanda, opening it, and promptly dumping leaves all over the floor.

With a big happy sigh, Catty rolled around on the leaves, ready for her zoomies to take over. Chef Wanda was a genius! Catty never considered putting catnip in spaghetti sauce before!

"Um, Catty?" Bebe asked as she and Chef Wanda towered over her, looking confused. Catty froze, and it was as if she'd been pulled out of a dream. Wait a minute. This didn't smell like catnip. Catty sat up. "This isn't . . . catnip?" she asked as her cheeks began to turn redder than the spaghetti sauce on the walls.

Bebe shook her head. "Just plain old oregano."

Chef Wanda stuttered, "I-I wouldn't say plain or old. That was premium heritage oregano from Istanbul . . . and now it's all over the floor."

Catty groaned as she stood up and cleaned herself off. "I'm so sorry. I've made such a mess of things."

"That's . . . that's quite all right, Catty," said Chef Wanda, but Catty wasn't sure she meant it.

"I think I should head home now," said Catty in a small voice, before Chef Wanda could reach for her own vacuum. "My mom is probably wondering where I am."

"But you just got here," Bebe said. "And you haven't even tried the cannoli we made!"

"I'm sure they're totally delicious," Catty said as she backed out of the kitchen, her face red. "I'll see you tomorrow in school, Bebe. Thank you for everything, Chef Wanda! And sorry again!" Catty took off, stumbling into her sneakers and then rushing down the sidewalk for home.

Who knew having best friends would be so *complicated*? She had to get home to a place where she was comfortable and could just be herself. A place without vacuums!

# CHAPTER SIX

When Catty got home, she was so relieved to see her sofa with its beloved claw marks, and Waffles waiting in the windowsill. Her house was just the right amount of messy, and just the right amount of *quiet*.

Catty kicked off her shoes—not because she had to, but because she wanted to—and then she face-planted on the sofa and sighed. "This is the life," she said.

"Catty, is that you?" Mom called as she walked in from the backyard, still wearing her work uniform. Like Catty, Mom was half-cat. She sat down in her special purple velvet armchair and began to scratch behind her ears. "How was school?"

Catty groaned into the sofa cushion.

"Could you translate that into words for me?" Mom asked.

Catty turned her head so that Mom could hear her. "I thought having friends was supposed to be great, but it's not. Have you ever been in the middle of two friends arguing? Or had a friend who talked too much or a friend who thought they were always right?" Catty sat up. "And other people's houses are the worst!

They smell weird. They're too messy or too clean. And the vacuums! So much vacuuming!"

"Oh, my sweet kitty-cat!" said Mom. "Friendships are complicated. Did I ever tell you about the time my friends pushed me into the pool at a pool party? I couldn't believe they didn't know how much cats hate water! And when your Granny Tabby went to a slumber party, her friend's mother put out a litter box for her because she didn't know what to make of a half-cat, half-girl.

Sometimes having friends means putting up with some uncomfortable compromises."

"I think I just need to be myself for a little while," Catty told Mom.

"Why don't you spend time with your Scratch Pad?" Mom suggested.

Now, that was a great idea!

With Waffles in one hand and her Scratch Pad in the other, Catty went out to the back patio—or catio, as Mom called it—and cozied up in a big wicker chair.

As she sat there under the warm sun, Catty flipped through the pages until she settled on an entry from Granny Tabby when she was a little girl.

Dear Diary,

I spent all day hiding from Ginger. I know she's my best friend. But sometimes her laugh makes me want to scratch a hole in a wall. She sounds like an angry bird and it makes my tail bristle every single time!

She's so funny and we have the best of times. But that laugh! It makes my toes curl and ears ring. And sometimes she even snorts! Last time,

she startled me so much that I nearly jumped into a tree.

I do feel bad, though. She always covers her mouth when she laughs, like she's a little embarrassed. I know she can't help it. And she is the funniest person I know, so I guess if my jokes were as good as hers, I'd laugh until I snorted too.

Maybe I just needed a break today . . . Come to think of it, I haven't laughed all day . . .

Hugs and Meows,

Tabby

PS. I can hear Ginger coming now and I'm pretty curious about what's *got her laughing this time. I'll report back.*

Catty sort of wished she could hear Ginger's laugh for herself and decide if it was as bad as Granny Tabby made it out to be. She couldn't help but think about Jo and how she always had something to say. And how Bebe could be a bit of a know-it-all . . .

Maybe having friends didn't mean never fighting or always agreeing. But maybe everyone was a little like Ginger. Her laugh got under Granny Tabby's claws, but she always had the best jokes. What if the things that made people a little annoying at times also made them special? Sure, Jo talked nonstop, but she knew a little something about everything! And Bebe could think she was always right, but a lot of the time, she was!

And there had to be things about Catty that drove Jo and Bebe up the wall, hadn't there?

There was one thing Catty knew for certain: Meatball Mania was tomorrow night, and she couldn't bear the idea of it being ruined because they couldn't stop the Gobbler Bandit . . . or whatever it was.

The fundraiser was on the line. Catty had to find out who or what was behind the mischief at school, and she couldn't do it alone.

# CHAPTER SEVEN

It was the night of the Meatball Mania spaghetti fundraiser, and Catty could practically taste the excitement. Maybe it was her Tail Intuition! Or just the smell of meatballs . . .

A few hours before the dinner, Catty changed into her special uniform: a white shirt, black pants, and a red bow tie. Then Mom and Dad drove Catty to school and dropped her off at the cafeteria.

"Good luck tonight!" Mom said, waving from the passenger window.

"We'll see you at the dinner!" called Dad.

"You'd better be hungry!" Catty said, and hurried inside to join the others.

All the volunteer students had lined up in the cafeteria, ready to wait tables. Catty spotted Jo standing in line and rushed over to join her. Jo's bow tie was a little more pink than red.

"I'm so excited," said Jo. "And nervous! Have you spotted anything suspicious?"

"Not yet," said Catty, "but my ears and nose are on high alert."

Mr. Grole cleared his throat and stood before the volunteers. He put on his most serious face and folded his hands behind his back. "All right, troops," he said. "Tonight's the big night. I've run three annual Meatball Manias and I haven't lost a single meatball yet, so listen up and do as I say, and we'll all get through this without stains on our shirts. Now, remember . . ." He held up three fingers to list the rules. "Don't put more on a tray than you can carry. Be sure to say 'Pardon me' when you reach over someone. And whatever you do, don't sneeze on the food!"

Catty wrinkled her nose. She'd definitely broken that last rule yesterday. The lingering smell of oregano made her tail twitch.

Mr. Grole clapped. "Okay, to your stations!"

"I think we're supposed to meet Bebe in the back," Jo said, and the two girls headed through the double doors to the kitchen.

What they found was kitchen chaos.

"My meatballs!" Chef Wanda screamed, with her apron covered in sauce. She didn't look nearly as neat and put together as she had yesterday. Her hair was standing straight up—and was that spaghetti in her hair? "We can't have a Meatball Mania without meatballs, and they're *missing*!"

Jo gasped. "Oh no! The Gobbler Bandit!"

Just then Bebe marched through the door, pulling Milo along with her.

"Whoa," said Milo, surveying the mess. "Isn't the pasta supposed to go *on* the plates and not *on* the floor?"

"What's *he* doing here?" Catty asked. There were already too many cooks in this kitchen, and now Milo was here too. For paws' sake!

"In case you haven't noticed, the mice have struck again!" Bebe said in a panic, looking as uncool as Catty had ever seen. "We need more manpower—or, uh, *kid*power."

Milo held up a bright red bag with DETECTIVE KIT in big black letters across the front. "I thought you three could use

someone with real skills."

Jo put her hands on her hips. "Just because you have a bag of toys doesn't mean you have real skills."

Milo let out a loud *hmph*. "They're not toys! They're tools!"

"Jo, Milo is here to help us actually solve this mystery before it gets any worse," Bebe said with her forehead furrowed. "At least he's not just standing around talking about some bandit who doesn't even exist!"

"Guys, please don't start fighting now," Catty begged, but Jo looked stricken.

"How dare—!"

"Um, a little help, please!" Chef Wanda yelled.

Four huge pots of spaghetti were boiling over as Chef Wanda raced to turn off the stove. Smoke was billowing from one of the ovens, along with the smell of burning bread.

Beside Catty, Bebe shrieked, Jo's jaw dropped, and Milo just went "Whoa" again. They were like mice in headlights!

Someone had to do something.

Catty pounced into action. "Bebe, you help with the spaghetti. Jo, check on that bread . . ."

The two girls nodded and rushed to help out.

"What about me?" Milo asked.

Catty frowned. She hated to ask Milo for help, but maybe that detective kit could be useful. "We're on the hunt for a thief," Catty told him. "Someone stole the meatballs, and we've got to get them back. I'll sniff them out while you use that bag of tricks to find some clues."

Milo nodded. "You know, you can be a little bossy."

Catty huffed. "Well, you can be a little rude. No one's purr-fect!"

Milo looked surprised, then laughed. "I guess that's true!"

"Come on, we've got to catch a meatball bandit," said Catty.

Milo opened his bag and took out a pair of reflective glasses with a light attached and an oversize magnifying glass. "These glasses have little mirrors on the inside of the lenses that help me see what's going on behind me. It's like I have eyes in the back of my head. Does your bushy tail do anything that cool?"

Catty grumbled at him and began to prowl. Prowling was like regular walking, but on all fours, and sneakier. It always helped her concentrate on smells when she could go into prowl mode.

Catty got low and closed her eyes. She sniffed, and snuffed, and did a big *snaaaaarf* . . . until she smelled something different, something that didn't belong. She followed the scent until it faded. Then she tried closing her eyes again.

Nothing about what was going on in the kitchen helped her concentration, either.

"Guests are arriving and ready to be served!" Mr. Grole called from the kitchen window.

"Chefs!" shouted Chef Wanda. "Spaghetti on plates, ASAP!"

"Yes, Chef!" Bebe and Jo called back.

Volunteer servers began to pile up at the kitchen door, their hands empty and waiting to serve.

"I need six plates with extra meatballs!" one server said.

"Right away!" said Chef Wanda. "Uh . . . as soon as we find them!"

"Look there!" said Milo to Catty. He was peering through his magnifying glass at the floor near the wall. "I think it's a food trail!"

Catty looked closely. Milo was right! There was a trail of food leading across the kitchen floor.

"Well," said Catty, hands on her hips. "I bet I *could* have spotted that." She couldn't help but smile at Milo's proud grin. "But good job."

"The trail disappears pretty quickly though," he added.

"That's all right. Now that I know which direction to look, I can find the scent again and track the thief that way!" said Catty.

She resumed her prowling, and sure enough, soon she could smell the same odd, earthy scent she'd smelled in Mrs. Macaw's classroom and Mr. Grole's snack pantry.

The food trailed in circles around the floor, under counters, behind appliances. Catty walked backwards, hoping the trail would lead the way, until she collided with something and jumped into the air, holding her tail tight.

When she landed on her feet, she spun around—and came face-to-face with a giant monstrous eye!

"Eeeeeep!" Catty screeched.

But the only thing standing in front of her was Milo with his magnifying glass held so close to his face that it made his eye five times its real size.

"Watch where you're going!" Milo said.

"I was just following the food trail!" she told him. But as Catty looked around at the path, she realized that the only place the food trail had led her was straight to Milo.

Jo and Bebe continued to bicker as a plate of spaghetti hit the ground, splattering sauce and pasta everywhere, including all over Catty's face.

Catty swiped her finger over her nose and then tasted the sauce. Yep, it definitely needed more catnip.

Chef Wanda looked like she was about to pull her hair out. "This is a disaster. My kitchen is one giant health code violation! And now we probably have mice! MICE!"

"The bread is burned!" Jo called out. "Like, scorched!"

"I think this spaghetti is overdone," Bebe

said, pulling a big gloppy spoonful of pasta out of the water. "We might need to start over, Mom—I mean, Chef."

"THAT'S IT!" shouted Chef Wanda. It was the loudest shout Catty had ever heard. Cats three towns over must have heard it.

Everyone got very quiet.

"This is chaos," said Chef Wanda. "Everybody out. Now."

# CHAPTER EIGHT

All Catty wanted was to slink away into hiding. She needed a break from all these harsh sounds and weird smells. Where was a cozy cat tree and ball of yarn when a feline needed one?

While Chef Wanda started cooking the pasta again for the waiting diners, the kids all scattered. Catty wove in and out of people and puddles of spaghetti sauce until she found herself at the doorway of a room full of boxes of canned food. So this was where the cafeteria's endless supply of green beans came from.

Sitting on top of a box, all by herself, was Bebe. Her shoulders were slumped and she wiped at her eyes like she might have been crying.

"I'm sorry," Catty said as she began to back out of the door. "I didn't think there was anyone in here."

"It's okay," Bebe told her. "We can have a pity party. Table for two, please."

Catty had really hoped to be alone, but the frenzy happening just around the corner forced her to step inside the storage room. With her tail practically dragging on the floor and her ears drooping, Catty sat on a stack of boxes beside Bebe and the two just stared at the ground and sighed. Neither of them knew quite what to say. It was always Jo who seemed to have the right words. Well, maybe not the right words, but *words* at the very least.

The door swung open and both girls' heads snapped up.

Jo stepped inside and shut the door behind her. She was out of breath and stood with her back against the door, like she was hiding from a whole gang of hungry zombies. "It's madness out there," she said.

"Well, it's pretty gloomy in here . . ." Catty said.

Jo frowned. "Yeah, you two aren't exactly looking like rays of sunshine."

Bebe crossed her arms and rolled her eyes.

"Do you have something to say?" Jo asked Bebe.

*Uh-oh*, Catty thought. This was quickly going from pity party to catfight.

"No," Bebe said. "Not all of us have something to say every moment of the day."

Jo threw her arms up as she stomped over and sat down between the two girls. "Do you think I don't know that I talk too much?" she asked.

"She didn't mean that," Catty said, feeling suddenly guilty for not trying to step in and fix things. But Bebe was a little bit right. Jo really did know how to talk.

"Sometimes my brain is just a jumble," Jo said. "Like it's a big knot and the only way I know how to untangle it is with my words."

"I love unraveling things," Catty said sympathetically.

"I guess that does make sense, Jo," Bebe agreed. "I hate when things are a mess."

Jo looked at them both. "And you're both so cool. Sometimes I think there's no way either of you could actually want to be friends with me. So I get nervous. And I jabber and then I get worried that I'm talking so much, but instead of stopping I just keep going."

"Of course we want to be friends with you," Bebe said. "And I'm sorry I've been so crabby lately. I get pretty grumpy when things are disorganized, so I'm sure you can imagine how I feel about the state of the cafeteria kitchen right now. It makes me more antsy than when someone takes my colored pencils out of alphabetical order, ya know?"

Jo and Catty were silently confused for a moment before Jo broke the silence with a laugh. "Actually, I totally don't know. But maybe it's good that you're so organized. You can keep me on task and I can help you loosen up a little bit."

Bebe smiled and wrapped an arm around Jo's shoulders as both girls looked at Catty.

It was obviously Catty's turn to share, but she felt bad saying how she really felt. Jo needed to think out loud and Bebe needed to keep things in order, but sometimes what Catty needed was to be alone. Would that hurt her friends' feelings?

Catty took a deep breath. If she wanted to make friends and keep them, she'd have to be honest about how she felt, even when it wasn't all warm and fuzzy.

"Sometimes I just need quiet," Catty admitted softly. "Sometimes all the noises make me feel all cattywampus, and not in a fun way. It's not that I don't like going to school or having friends, but it's really easy for the cat side of me to get a little hissy when it gets to be too much."

"That makes sense," Bebe said. "I don't hiss, but sometimes I feel like I could."

"I could use some practice learning how to be quiet," Jo said. "Maybe we could start now."

Bebe shrugged and nodded. "It's worth a try!"

"A moment of silence?" Jo whispered solemnly.

Catty grinned. "That would be great."

The girls quietly sat shoulder to shoulder, and it was so nice and still that Catty could practically fall asleep.

Until . . . wait a minute . . .

"Do you guys hear that noise?" Catty whispered. She closed her eyes to concentrate a little more.

"Is it coming from under the floor?" Bebe asked.

Catty's eyes widened and her tail bristled. "Are those . . . paws?"

# CHAPTER NINE

"Time to pounce!" Catty yelled back at Bebe and Jo as she raced out the storage room door. "I hear someone . . . or something!"

The three girls hurried through the kitchen and out of the cafeteria with Milo close at their heels.

"What's going on?" Milo asked as everyone followed Catty down the hallway. She was focused on the scratching noise she'd heard, like she was following a laser pointer. And now she swore she could smell something too . . . Was that a wet dog she smelled? Surely she'd know if a dog was sneaking into the school.

Catty followed her sense of smell and hearing right through the auditorium to the basement door behind the stage. The sounds and scent were just as clear to her as the food trail had been in the kitchen.

"Wait a minute," Bebe said just as Catty reached for the rusty old door. "That place is going to be covered in dust and cobwebs. I really don't want to get messy when we still have to help out at Meatball Mania, especially when Chef Wanda is already freaking out."

Catty looked down at her spaghetti sauce-stained shirt. "Um, speak for yourself, but I think it's a little too late for me."

She began to open the door when Jo pulled it shut.

"No way, it's too dark down there. Plus, I've heard the basement is haunted, and if I were a ghost who got stuck hunting an elementary school for all of eternity, I don't think I'd be very friendly."

"You're such a scaredy-cat," Milo told her.

Bebe rolled her eyes at him.

"You can hold my hand, Jo," Catty said. "And, Bebe, I promise that I'll find you a new apron if you get dirty, okay?"

Jo and Bebe looked at each other, and even though they seemed unsure, they both nodded.

"Does anyone want to know what *I* think?" asked Milo.

"No," all three girls said in unison as Catty opened the door and they began to walk down the long creaky staircase.

The door shut behind them and they were in near darkness except for a small light downstairs. Milo let out a little *meep.*

"Who's the scaredy-cat now?" Jo asked Milo.

He grumbled but said nothing else as Catty bravely led the way.

When she stepped down from the last step, she turned the corner and froze. Jo, Bebe, and Milo quickly piled up behind her.

"Hey, what's the holdup?" Milo demanded, until he peered over Catty's shoulder and saw what exactly had her frozen in place.

There in the far corner of the room was the roundest raccoon Catty had ever seen. He sat on a throne made of random objects like broken rackets and discarded toys. He wore a metal crown that looked like it had been made from an empty food can, as if he were a king.

And around his neck was a macaroni necklace.

The raccoon king paused with one meatball in each paw. He'd been caught red-handed—literally! The furry little guy let the meatballs fall to the ground, as if that somehow made him less guilty.

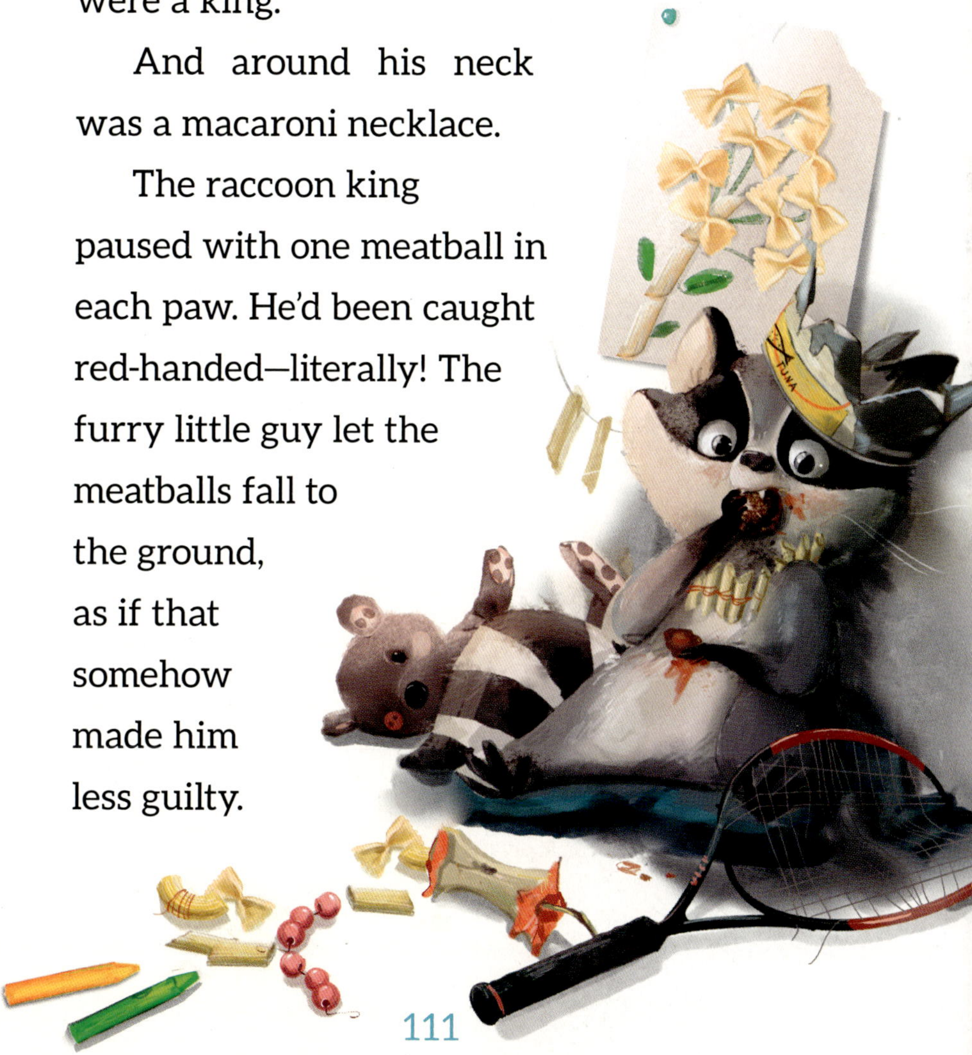

"Well, he's no Gobbler Bandit, but he is kind of cute," Jo said.

"And he's definitely bigger than a mouse," Bebe admitted.

"Uhhh, I'm out of here," Milo said. "That raccoon is as big as me!"

"Hey, check it out," Bebe said. "Looks like he's a fan of our work."

They glanced up and saw that the walls of the raccoon's den were covered in partially eaten macaroni art, stuck up with chewed gum and Silly Putty.

Catty stepped toward the raccoon. He didn't *seem* scary. In fact, with his big round eyes, he seemed lonely, and reminded Catty of how she felt before school, before meeting her friends.

"I like your crown," Catty said.

The raccoon touched his crown as if he were a bit embarrassed by it now. He lowered his head almost like he was bowing.

"He must be a pretty hungry little guy," Jo said.

The raccoon's stomach let out a long, low grumble.

All three girls laughed, and the raccoon covered his eyes, like he couldn't believe how noisy his tummy had been.

"I get a little embarrassed when my stomach growls too," Catty told him.

He pulled his hands away and picked up a half-eaten meatball to give to her.

Catty smiled. "I'm not hungry right now, thank you." She didn't bother mentioning that eating a half-eaten meatball from a raccoon wasn't exactly appetizing.

"What do we do?" asked Bebe. "I don't want to take food away from him, but we can't let him steal food right out from under everyone's noses."

Catty nodded, but she didn't know the solution.

"Wait a minute," Jo chimed in. "Raccoons are scavengers, right? They love leftovers!"

The raccoon held his hand to his forehead like he could faint with delight.

That was it! Leftovers! "Mr. Raccoon? Or Raccoon? Or Raccoon King? I don't know what to call you . . ."

The raccoon pointed to his hat.

"Raccoon King it is!" Catty said. "How about we make a deal, Your Majesty? You'll stop stealing our food—and art—before anyone has a chance to enjoy it, and we will bring you all of our best leftovers every day after lunch. Bebe's mom is a chef, so I can guarantee she's got the good stuff."

"And my mom lets me pack whatever I want. So, if I want a pickle peanut butter sandwich, no one's stopping me!" Jo told him.

Raccoon King's eyes practically turned into hearts at the mention of pickle peanut butter sandwiches. The thought made Catty a little queasy, but the heart wanted what the heart wanted!

"Do we have a deal?" Catty asked.

The raccoon crossed his little arms over his chest and walked back and forth for a moment before holding out a paw for Catty to shake.

"It's a deal!" Catty said. "And if you're a fan of art, we'd love to make you some more."

"Totally," Bebe agreed, "but if we're going to do that, we need to get back to this fundraiser so we can make enough money to buy all the supplies we need!"

Raccoon King sat back on his throne with his half-eaten meatball, and Catty, Jo, and Bebe gave him quick curtsies before racing back up the stairs.

The meatballs were a lost cause, but at least the girls could still help Chef Wanda in the kitchen. She'd be relieved to know there was no mouse problem! But maybe a Raccoon King wasn't that much better.

The girls decided it was best for them to keep that part to themselves.

# CHAPTER TEN

By the time the girls made it back to the kitchen, the situation hadn't improved much. Which was why Chef Wanda nearly cried when she saw her assistants return.

"Oh, girls!" she said. "Everything is just one big mess."

"There's no such thing as a mess that can't be cleaned up," Catty told her with determination.

"Amen to that," Bebe agreed.

Someone needed to get things under control, and fast!

"Jo," Catty said, "how about you go talk to the guests out in the cafeteria and keep them entertained? And maybe let them know that the meatballs are off the menu."

Jo nodded. "I've been training my whole life for this moment!"

"And, Bebe!" Catty exclaimed. "If there's anyone who can get this mess organized in a hurry, it's you. Let your neat freak side do all the talking!"

Bebe stared at Catty with a blank expression. It was like she couldn't believe that someone was encouraging her to be a know-it-all.

"Well, hop to it!" Catty said.

That seemed to snap Bebe out of her daze. She pointed to Catty. "I need you to get all the volunteer waiters organized into one line with a list of exactly what they need."

"You got it, boss lady!" Catty loved to see her friends lean in to what made them each special.

Bebe hustled over to her mom and helped her calm down and get the food in order. Even without the meatballs, it all looked so delicious. She couldn't wait to share the leftovers with her new friend.

Catty began herding all the volunteers into one line like they were a bunch of little kittens. She helped them each organize their orders while Jo talked up a storm, charming every single table one by one. By the time the food started to come out, most people were so hungry they were ready to eat the napkins! Catty wondered if they even tasted the dinner, they scarfed it so fast.

After the dinner was over, Mr. Grole had them sit down in the cafeteria. "Well, I've got bad news and good news, everyone."

Catty held her breath. Had they not raised enough money? The place was packed. How could that be? Catty looked to her friends, who both shrugged.

"The bad news," Mr. Grole continued, "is that we still haven't found the missing meatballs."

The students groaned in unison.

Catty, Jo, and Bebe smiled at each other.

"But the good news is that no one seemed to care! We raised more than enough money to replenish our art supplies!"

Catty jumped up and began to cheer just as the students erupted in celebration. It was so loud, but this time Catty didn't mind one bit.

When it was time to leave, Catty walked by her classroom and noticed something shiny in her cubby. On the top shelf was a very interesting surprise: A small metal crown made from an empty can of tomatoes.

Catty put on the crown and wore it home. She displayed it on her bookshelf right next to all of her most prized possessions.

Then she curled up in her favorite cat tree with Waffles.

Alone at last!

Dear Diary,

Turns out the bandit was just a very classy Raccoon King with an appreciation of the arts. Who would've thought? I guess we were all wrong.

But there's no way we would've solved this mystery and made ~~Meatball Mania~~ Spaghetti Night a huge success without Bebe's organizational skills and the power of Jo's chatter. And I guess if I didn't need a little bit of quiet

sometimes, I never would have heard the sound of the Raccoon King's little paws scratching.

I can't wait to see all the new art supplies and maybe even use them to make a portrait of our new resident raccoon.

Peace, Love & Claws,

Catty

## Also by Julie Murphy

*Catty Corner Lands on Her Feet*

union square kids
NEW YORK

UNION SQUARE KIDS and the distinctive Union Square Kids logo
are trademarks of Union Square & Co., LLC.

Union Square & Co., LLC, is a subsidiary of Sterling Publishing Co., Inc.



ISBN 978-1-4549-5649-5 (hardcover)
ISBN 978-1-4549-5650-1 (paperback)
ISBN 978-1-4549-5876-5 (e-book)

Library of Congress Cataloging-in-Publication Data

Names: Murphy, Julie, author. | Farb, Eve, illustrator.
Title: Catty Corner pounces into action / by Julie Murphy ; illustrated by Eve Farb.
Description: New York : Union Square Kids, 2025. | Series: Catty corner | Audience: Ages 4-8. | Summary: "Catty and her friends must solve the missing snacks problem at school."— Provided by publisher.
Identifiers: LCCN 2024022372 (print) | LCCN 2024022373 (ebook) | ISBN 9781454956495 (hardcover) | ISBN 9781454956501 (paperback) | ISBN 9781454958765 (epub)
Subjects: CYAC: Cats—Fiction. | Schools—Fiction. | Problem solving—Fiction. | Mice—Fiction.
Classification: LCC PZ7.M95352 Cd 2025 (print) | LCC PZ7.M95352 (ebook) | DDC [Fic]—dc23
LC record available at https://lccn.loc.gov/2024022372
LC ebook record available at https://lccn.loc.gov/2024022373

For information about custom editions, special sales, and premium purchases, please contact specialsales@unionsquareandco.com.

Printed in China

Lot #:

2 4 6 8 10 9 7 5 3 1

11/24

unionsquareandco.com

Cover and interior design by Amelia Mack
Cover and interior art by Eve Farb